THE
BORROWED
HOUSE

BY

MARY
ROBERTS
RINEHART

BLACKBIRD BOOKS
NEW YORK • LOS ANGELES

A Blackbird Classic, March 2024

Manufactured in the United States of America.

The events and characters depicted in this book are
fictional.

Cataloging-in-Publication Data

Rinehart, Mary Roberts.
The borrowed house / Mary Roberts Rinehart.
p. cm.
1. Suffragists—Fiction.
2. Suffragists—Great Britain—Fiction.
3. England—Social life and customs—
20th century—Fiction. I. Title.
PS3535.I73 B67 2024 813'.54—dc23 2024931826

Blackbird Books
www.bbirdbooks.com
email us at editor@bbirdbooks.com

ISBN 978-1-61053-049-1

First Blackbird Edition

10 9 8 7 6 5 4 3 2 1

THE
BORROWED
HOUSE

I

"And the things the balloon man said!" observed Daphne, stirring her tea. Daphne is my English cousin, and misnamed. "He went too high and Poppy's nose began to bleed."

"It poured," Poppy confirmed plaintively to me. "I leaned over the edge of the basket and it poured. And the next day, the papers said it had rained blood in Tooting and that quantities of people had gone to the churches!" Poppy is short and wears her hair cut close and curled with an iron all over her head. She affects plaids.

"Then," Daphne went on, addressing the room in general, "he let some gas out of the bag and we began to settle. But just when we were directly over the Tower, he grew excited and threw out sand. He said he wasn't going to hang his balloon on the Houses of Parliament like a penny ornament on a Christmas tree. And then the wind carried us north and we missed it altogether."

Mrs. Harcourt-Standish took a tea cake. "I was seasick," she remarked pensively, "and he was unpleasant about that, too. It was really mountain sickness, although, of course, there wasn't any mountain. When we began to throw out the handbills, he asked if I had swallowed *them,* too."

Mrs. Harcourt-Standish plays up the feminine. She is slim and blond, and wears slinky clothes and a bang—only they call it a fringe—across her forehead. She has been in prison five times and is supposed to have influence with the Cabinet. She showed me a lot of photographs of herself in the dock and in jail, put up in a frame that was made to represent a barred window. It was Violet Harcourt-Standish, you remember, who broke up the meeting of the Woman's Liberty League, the rival Suffragette association, by engaging the suite below their rooms, burning chemicals in the grates, and sending in a fire alarm when the smoke poured out of the windows.

I had been in England visiting Daphne for four months while Mother went to Italy, and I had had a very queer time. One was apt to go shopping with Daphne and end up on a carriage block or the box of a hansom cab, passing out handbills about votes for women. And once, when we dressed in our best gowns and went to a reception for the Cabinet, or something of the kind, Daphne stood on the stairs and began to make a speech. It turned out that she hadn't been invited at all, and they put her out immediately—politely, but firmly. I slid away into the crowd, quite pale with the shock and disgrace, and stood in a corner, waiting to be arrested, and searched for the spoons. But for a long time, no one noticed me. Then a sunburned gentleman who was passing in the crowd saw me, hesitated, and came back.

"I beg pardon," he said, and my heart turned entirely over, "but I think you came with Miss Wyndham? If you will allow me—"

"I am afraid you have made a mistake," I replied frigidly, with my lips stiff with fright. He bowed at that and passed on, but not before he had looked straight into my eyes and read the lie there.

After ages I left the window where I had taken shelter and got somehow to the dressing room. Of course, Daphne had taken the carriage, so I told a sad-eyed maid that I was ill and would not wait for my brougham, and to call a cab. I was perfectly numb with rage when I got to Daphne's apartment, and burst in like a whirlwind. But Daphne was not at home. She came in at three that morning, maudlin with triumph, and found me asleep on the floor in my ball gown, with a half-packed trunk before me.

She brought me tea and toast herself the next morning and offered it on her knees, which means something for Daphne—she is very stout and almost unbendable—and explained that I had been her patent of respectability, and that it had been a coup; that Mrs. Langley, of the Woman's Liberty League, had hired as a maid for the reception and had never got her foot out of the dressing room! Red hair? Yes. And when I told Daphne that Mrs. Langley had helped me into my wrap, she got up heavily and hopped three steps one way and three another, which is the way Daphne dances with joy.

I am afraid I have digressed. It is much harder to write a thing than to tell it. I used to write stories for our Journal at school, and the girls were mad over them. But they were love stories, and this one deals with English politics and criminals—yes, you might call it a crime story. Of course there is love, too, but it comes in rather unexpectedly.

I left Daphne hopping three steps each way in triumph. Well, after that, she did not take me around with her, although her friends came in and talked about The Cause to me quite often. And gradually, I began to see that there was something to it, and why, if I paid taxes, shouldn't I vote? And hadn't I as much intelligence as the cab drivers and street sweepers? And why couldn't I will my money to my children if I ever had any?—children, not money. Of course, as Father pointed out afterward, I should have been using my abilities in America; but most of the American women I knew were so cravenly and abjectly contented. But even after my conversion, Daphne would not take me in the balloon. She said I represented too much money to risk dumping in the Thames or hanging on a chimney.

The meeting at Daphne's was mainly to talk over the failure of the balloon ascension and to plan something new. But the actual conspiracy that followed was really an accident. It came about in the most casual way.

Violet Harcourt-Standish got up and went to the mirror to put on her veil, and some of the people began to gather their wraps.

"I'm tired," Daphne said suddenly. "We don't seem to get anywhere. We always come out the door we go in."

"Sometimes forcibly," Poppy said to me aside.

"And I haven't been strong, you know, since last summer," Daphne went on. Everybody nodded sympathetically. Daffie had raised a disturbance when Royalty was laying a cornerstone and had been jailed for it. (They put her to making bags and she sewed "Votes for Women" in white thread on every bag she made.) "I am going to take Madge down to Ivry for a week." I am Madge.

Violet turned from the mirror and raised her eyebrows. "Ivry!" she said. "How familiar it sounds! Do you remember, Daphne, when pressure at the Hall became too strong for me, how I used to ride over to Ivry and have hysterics in the Tudor Room? And how once I wept on your Louis-Seize divan and had to have the purple stains bleached off my face? You lived a sort of vicarious matrimonial existence in those days, didn't you?"

Whatever she may have done to the Louis-Seize divan in earlier days, she was cheerful enough now, and I hailed her with delight.

"Do you live near Ivry?" I exclaimed. "How jolly! That is English; I am frightfully English in my speech after a few weeks in London."

Somebody laughed, and Daphne chuckled. It isn't especially feminine to chuckle, but neither is Daphne.

"My dear child," Mrs. Harcourt-Standish said, turning to me, "Harcourt Hall is closed. Mr. Harcourt is no longer my husband. The one is empty, the other in Canada"—vague, but rhetorical—"I have forgotten them both." There was nothing ambiguous about that. "I recall the house as miles from everything that was joyful. I shall always regard my being taken there as nothing short of kidnapping."

Then—she stopped short and glanced at Daphne. From Daphne, her eyes travelled to Ernestine Sutcliffe, who put down her teacup with a clatter. There was a sudden hushed silence in the room; then Lady Jane Willoughby, who had been tying her motor veil, took it off and folded it in her lap. The Staffords, Poppy and her mother, exchanged glances. Without in the least understanding it, I saw that something psychological was happening.

"Why not?" said Daphne quietly, looking around. "The house is still furnished, isn't it, Violet? And I suppose you could get in?"

Violet shrugged her shoulders. "I dare say; as I recall it, one could enter any one of the doors by merely leaning against it. The place is a million years old."

Everybody talked at once for a few minutes. I gave up trying to understand and took a fresh tea cake. Then I noticed Lady Willoughby. In all that militant body, whatever adventure was afoot, hers was the only craven soul. She was picking at her veil with nervous fingers.

"I—don't you think it is very radical?" she ventured when she could be heard. Here Mrs. Stafford objected to the word "radical," and she substituted "revolutionary." "I should not wish anything to happen to him. He was a great friend of Willoughby's mother while she lived."

"That's all right among ourselves, Jane," Mrs. Stafford put in, "but if I recall the circumstances, I wouldn't lay any emphasis on *that*. Anyhow, we don't intend to murder the man."

Lady Jane was only partially reassured. "Of course, you wouldn't mean to," she retorted, "but there is no use asking me to forget what Poppy Stafford did to the president of the Board of Trade last summer."

Poppy glanced up and shook her curls. "You are envious, Willieboy," she said, and put four lumps of sugar in her tea. "Willieboy" is Lady Willoughby's affectionate diminutive. They had started the tea all over again and I rather edged away from Poppy, but Daphne said afterward it was only a matter of a chair Poppy threw from the gallery at a public meeting, and that the man it fell on was only a secretary to the president of the Board of Trade.

Finally, I made out what the plan was, and mentally, during the rest of the meeting, I was making bags in jail.

They were going to abduct the Prime Minister!

Lady Jane had stopped looking back and had put her hand to the plow. (This sounds well, so I won't cut it out; but wasn't it Lot's wife that looked back? And wasn't that before the day of plows? Or was it?) And it was she who finally settled the whole thing, for it seems that the P. M. had confided to Lord Willoughby that the town was so noisy with Suffragettes that he could not find a quiet spot for a rubber of bridge; that since the balloon incident, he slept in his clothes with the windows shut and locked; and that since the latest kitchen maid had turned out to be the Honourable Maude Twombley, who slipped handbills into his entrées and served warnings in his dessert, he was going to travel, incognito and alone, to his daughter's place, The Oaks, outside of West Newbury, and get a little sleep.

And West Newbury was only four miles from the empty Harcourt Hall! In short, as Daphne succinctly put it: "Our Jonah was about to jump voluntarily overboard from the ship of state into the whaleboned jaws of the Suffragette whale."

Everybody went mad at that point, but as they grew excited, I got cold. It began with my toes and went all over me.

Ernestine Sutcliffe stood on one of Daphne's tulipwood and marquetry chairs and made a speech, gesticulating with her cup and dripping tea on me. And then somebody asked me to stand up and say what I thought. (I have never really spoken in public, but I always second the motions in a little club I belong to at home. It is a current-events club—so much easier to get the news that way than to read the newspaper.)

So I got up and made a short speech. I said: "I am only a feeble voice in this clamour of outraged womanhood against the oppressor, Man. I believe in the franchise for women, the ballot instead of the ballet. But at home, in America, when we want to take a bath we don't jump off the Brooklyn Bridge into the East River to do it."

Then I sat down. Daphne was raging.

"You are exceedingly vulgar," she said, "but since you insist on that figure of speech, you in America have waited a long time for the bath, and if you continue your present methods you won't get it before you need it."

II

Now that they had thought of it, they were all frantic for fear Mrs. Cobden-Fitzjames and the Woman's Liberty League might think of it too, kidnap the Prime Minister, and leave us a miserable president of the Local Government Board or a wretched under-secretary of something or other.

The plan we evolved before the meeting broke up was to send a wire to Mrs. Gresham, the Premier's daughter, that he had been delayed, and to meet a later train. Then, Daphne's motor would meet the proper train—he was to arrive somewhere between seven and eight in the evening—carry his Impressiveness to Harcourt Hall and deliver him

into the hands of the enemy. As Violet Harcourt-
Standish voiced it: the motor gone, the railway miles
away, what can he do? He will keep awake, because
he will have slept in the train going down, and we
can give him a cold supper. Nothing heavy to make
him drowsy. Perhaps it would be better not to give
him anything. (Hear! Hear!) Then, six speeches, each
an hour long. At the end of that time we can promise
him something to eat and a machine to take him to
West Newbury on one condition. Everyone looked
up. "He must sign an endorsement of Suffrage for
Women." (Loud applause.)

"Why not have a table laid," I suggested, "and
show it to him? Let him smell it, so to speak. Visualise
your temptation. You know,—'And the devil—'"

"This is the Prime Minister, Madge," Daphne
broke in shortly, "and you are not happy in your
Scriptural references."

Things went along with suspicious smoothness.
Daphne really took the onus of the whole thing,
and, of course, I helped her.

We all got new clothes, for everybody knows
that if you can attract a man's eye you can get and
maybe hold his ear. And Daphne wrote a fresh
speech, one she had thought out in jail. It began,
"Words! Words!! Words!!!" She wrote a poem, too,

called *The Song of the Vote,* with the meter of *The Song of the Shirt,* and she wanted me to recite it, but even before I read it, I refused.

The gown Mother had ordered for me at Paquin's, on her way to the Riviera, came just in time, a nice white thing over silver, with a square-cut neck and bits of sleeves made of gauze and silver fringe. Daphne got a pink velvet, although she is stout and inclined to be florid. She had jet butterflies embroidered over it, a flight of them climbing up one side of her skirt and crawling to the opposite shoulder, so that if one stood off at a distance she had a curiously diagonal appearance, as if she had listed heavily to one side.

By hurrying, we got to Ivry on Thursday evening, and I was in a blue funk. Daphne was militantly cheerful, and, in the drawing room after dinner, she put the finishing touches to her speech. It was warm and rainy, and I wandered aimlessly around, looking at hideous English photographs and wondering if picking oakum in an English jail was worse than making bags—and if they could arrest me, after all. Could they touch an American citizen? (But was I an American citizen? Perhaps I should have been naturalised, or something of that kind!) And I thought of Mother at Florence, in the villa on the Via Michelangelo—Mother, who classes Suffragists with Anti-Vaccinationists and Theosophists.

I would have gone up to bed, but that meant a candle and queer, shaky shadows on the wall; so I stayed with Daphne and looked at the picture of a young man in a uniform.

"Basil Harcourt," Daphne said absently, with a pen in her mouth, when I asked about it. "Taken years ago, before he became an ass. How do you spell supererogation?"

"I haven't an idea," I admitted. "I don't even know what it means. I always confuse it with elee-mosynary." Daphne grunted. "Do you mean that this is Violet's husband?"

"It was—her first. Don't ask me about him: he always gives me indigestion. The man's mad! He stood right in this room, where he had eaten my ginger cakes all his life, and where he came to show me his first Eton collar and long trousers, and told me that he expected The Cause for his wife to be himself, and if she would rather raise hell for women than a family of children, she would have to choose at once. And Violet stood just where you are, Madge, and retorted that maternity was not a Cause, and that any hen in the barnyard could raise a family.

" 'I suppose you want to crow,' Basil said furiously, and slammed out. He went to Canada very soon after."

"Then perhaps he won't like our using his house for such a purpose. If he isn't in sympathy—"

"Twaddle," Daphne remarked, poising her pen to go on. "In the first place, it isn't a house—it's a rattletrap; and in the second place, he won't know a thing about it."

It was all very tragic. I was thinking of them when I went out on the terrace in Daphne's mackintosh. The air was damp and sticky, but it was better than Daphne's conversation. I stood in the fountain court, leaning against a column and listening to the spray as it blew over on to the caladium leaves.

I am not sure just when I saw the figure. First it was part of the gloom, a deeper shadow in the misty garden. I saw it, so to speak, out of the tail of my eye. When I looked directly, there was nothing there. Finally, I called softly over my shoulder to Daphne, but she did not hear. Instead, the shadow disengaged itself, moved forward, and resolved into Bagsby, Daphne's chauffeur.

"I wasn't sure at first that you saw me, Miss," he said, touching his cap. "It's my turn until midnight; Clarkson 'as it until three, and the gardener until daylight."

"Good gracious!" I gasped. "Do you mean you are guarding the house?"

"Perhaps it's more what you would call surveillance," he said cautiously, "the picture gallery being over your head, Miss, and an easy job from the conservatory roof. We 'aven't told Miss Wyndham, yet, Miss, but the Wimberley Romney was stolen from the Towers last night, Miss, and the whole countryside is up."

"The Romney?" I inquired. "Do you mean a painting?"

"Yes, Miss," he said patiently. "Cut out of its frame, and worth twenty thousand pounds! By a gentlemanly-looking chap—a tourist by appearances, with a bicycle, in tweeds and knickers, Miss."

Whether the bicycle or the tourist wore tweeds and knickers was not entirely clear. Bagsby was saying that the thief was supposed to be hiding on the moor when Daphne came out, and he disappeared.

Poppy Stafford and Ernestine came unexpectedly late that night, after I had gone to bed. I was in my first sleep and dreaming that Poppy was braining Bagsby with a gilt-framed painting, and that he was shouting "Votes for Women" instead of "'elp!" when somebody knocked at my door. It turned out to be Poppy, and she said she thought there was a bat in her room, and, as she was quite pallid with fright, I let her get into my bed. I was full of my dream, and I wanted to ask her some particulars about the man she had brained the summer before. But she put her head under the sheet, and as soon as she stopped trembling, she went to sleep.

Daphne called me early and we went over to the Hall to take a look around. As Daphne said, it would be night and the grounds would not matter, but we would have to uncover some of the furniture. And, as we could not let the servants know, we had to do it ourselves. We took a brush and pan, and tore up a linen sheet to dust with. Bagsby, who had been bribed, and suspected what he wasn't told, got the brush and pan, and later he showed us a pail and a piece of soap in the tonneau.

The place was dreadful. No doubt the park had been lovely, but it was overshadowed and overgrown. The hedges were untrimmed; paths began, wandered around, and died in a mess of undergrowth; and the terrace had lost an end in a wilderness where a garden house was falling to decay. The fading outlines of the kitchen garden seemed to shout aloud of lost domesticity, and over everything, lay a sodden layer of the previous autumn's leaves. (For fear I am accused of plagiarism, the sentence about the kitchen garden is not original. Madge.)

Daphne had got a key somewhere, and inside, it was worse. Coverings over the pictures and furniture, six years' dust everywhere, and a smell of mould like a crypt of one of the Continental cathedrals, only not so ancestor-y. While we were taking off the covers, with Bagsby's help, Daphne alternately sang and coughed in the dust.

"Why aren't you more cheerful?" she demanded. "It will be a red-letter day for The Cause. When I think of Mabel Fitzjames, I almost weep!"

"I think it must be because I am not used to it," I said meekly. "You see, I come from a Republican country—and Democratic, too, of course—and we don't have any Prime Ministers to steal. One has to grow accustomed to things like this gradually, Daffie, or be born to them. And then—I lay awake most of last night, wondering what would happen if he didn't—er—see the joke, you know."

Daphne jerked a cover from a moth-eaten sofa and sneezed promptly in the dust.

"Joke!" she repeated when she could speak. "No, I don't think he will see the joke. In fact, I don't believe he will think there is any joke to see. If I know anything, he is going to be wild. He's going to tear his hair and throw the vases off the mantel. He's going to use language that you never heard—at least, I hope not."

It was then that I realised that I was not, heart and soul, a Suffragist. If I had only had the courage to have spoken up then, to have told her that I didn't feel The Cause the way I ought to, and that I hoped to get married and have dozens of children, and that, anyhow, I had a headache, and I thought I ought to go on to Italy and meet Mother! But, instead, I followed her around like a sheep, tacking up cards with Suffrage mottoes on them all over the drawing room, and stretching a long canvas banner in the hall across the back of a great Gothic hall seat, with "Votes for Women" in red letters on it.

Bagsby brushed out a sort of oasis in the middle of the drawing room and a path to the door, and Daphne and I dusted seven chairs and a table. We had brought over a duplex lamp and some candles, and when we had put a cover on the table, the middle of the room looked quite habitable. Then Bagsby brushed the leaves off the steps, and, as Daphne pleasantly expressed it:

> *Won't you step into my parlor?*
> *Said the spider to the fly.*

Mrs. Stafford, Violet, and Lady Jane arrived that afternoon, after having waited to send the wire on which the conspiracy was hung. They put themselves into negligees and the hands of their maids at once, and were still dressing when Ernestine and I, the advance guard, started with the hamper of cold supper at half after six. Things went wrong from that moment.

Ernestine started to recite her speech to me as we went down the drive, found she had forgotten everything but the first sentence, which began, like *The Walrus and the Carpenter*, "The time has come—" and had to go back for the manuscript. We had to leave her for the second trip. Bagsby, who was in the conspiracy to the extent of five pounds, took me over alone and lighted the duplex lamp. He cut the telephone wire, also, by Daphne's order, before he left. We were not leaving anything to chance, although the thing had probably been disconnected for years.

"I 'ardly like to leave you 'ere alone, Miss," he said when everything was ready. It was growing dark by that time and raining again. "Folks is always ready to give a hempty 'ouse a black eye, so to speak. The 'all ghost isn't what you might call authenticated, but the 'ouse isn't 'abitable for a lady alone, Miss."

"I am not at all nervous," I quavered, as he went down the steps. "Only—please tell them to hurry, Bagsby."

I called to him again as he climbed into the car.

"Oh, Bagsby," I said nervously, "I—I suppose there is no danger of the picture thief being around."

"Not for pictures, anyhow, Miss," he returned jocularly, and started off.

Not for pictures, anyhow!

I stood at the door and watched the tail light of the motor disappear down the drive, show for an instant a spark by the dilapidated lodge, and then go out entirely.

*　　*　　*　　*　　*

The second part of the story begins about here. The first part, as you have seen, has been purely political: the rest is romance, intermingled with crime. It is a little late to bring in a hero, but to have done it earlier would have spoiled the story, besides being distinctly untruthful. And I suppose a real novelist would have had the hero turn out to be the sunburned gentleman of some pages before; but the fact is he wasn't, and I never saw the sunburned gentleman again.

Well, after Bagsby left, and I had examined the supper in the hamper and lighted more candles in the drawing room, I began to wish we had not cut the telephone wire so soon. It was perfectly dark, and anyone could step in through the windows— open to air the house—and cut my throat and take my string of pearls, which Father had had matched for me, and walk away calmly and be safe ten feet from the house in the undergrowth. And then Bagsby's ghost began to walk in my mind, and I quite lost sight of the fact that it was not authenticated.

It was blowing by that time, and every joint of the rheumatic old house creaked and groaned. The candles flickered and nearly went out, and the motto cards began to fly around the room as if carried by invisible fingers. One of them said, "You have been weighed and found wanting," and another one, "Beware!" They had all the effect of spirit messages on me. When I tried to close the windows, I found them stuck in their dilapidated frames. I wanted desperately to hide in a corner behind one of the high-backed chairs, but it was dusty there, and hardly dignified for a person who was abducting the Prime Minister. And then it would be ignominious to faint there and have someone peer over the back and say: "Why, here she is!"

So, to divert my mind from ghosts and gentle-
men burglars who steal pictures, I began to
investigate the hamper. There were sandwiches and
salad and pâté and quite a lot of stuff. But all at
once, I remembered that Daphne had given me the
small silver and that I had laid it on my bed and left
it there. And most of the provisions were too messy
for a P.M. to manage with his fingers. Luckily, I remembered something Violet had said when Daphne
gave me the silver.

"Personally," she had announced, "I am not in
favor of feeding him at all. Or else I would give him
prison fare. But if you're going to be mushy over
him, you'll probably find some dishes and forks in a
little closet over the dining room fireplace. They
were kept there to use if Basil ever went down for
the shooting, and I dare say they are still there."

So I picked up a candle and trembled through
the darkness toward where the breakfast room ought
to be. I went through a square garden hall which
shook when I did, and the motor coat around my
shoulders made the shadow of a pirate on the wall.

I found the breakfast room and the mantel cupboard at last, and, putting the candle on a chair,
stood for a moment listening, my hands clapped over
my heart. I thought I heard someone walking over

bare boards nearby, but the sounds, whatever they were, ceased.

The mantel cupboard was locked. I pulled and twisted at the knob to no purpose. Finally, I dug at the lock with a hairpin, and something gave; the door swung open with a squeak, and a moment later, I had a flannel case in my hands and was taking out some silver forks. At that moment, a plate in the cupboard fell forward with a slam, and something leaped on to the forks, which I dropped with a crash. The candle went out immediately, and, gasping for breath, I backed against the cupboard and stood staring into the blackness of the room.

The door by which I had entered was a faint, yellowish rectangle from the distant hall lamp. That is, it had been a rectangle. It was partly obscured now. And gradually the opacity took on the height and breadth and general outline of a man. He was pointing a revolver at me!

III

I think it occurred to him then that I might be pointing something at him—not knowing that my deadliest weapon was a silver fork. For he slid inside the room with his back against the wall. And there we stood, backed against opposite corners, staring into the darkness, and I, for one, totally unable to speak. Finally, he said: "I think it will end right here."

"I—I don't know what you mean," I quavered, for I was plainly expected to say something. There was another total silence, which I learned afterward was inability on *his* part to speak. Then—

"By Jove!" he exclaimed; and then again, under his breath: "By Jove!"

(That assured me somewhat. "By Jove" is so largely a gentleman's exclamation. If he had said "Blow me," which is English lower class, or "Shiver my timbers," I know I should have shivered mine. But "By Jove" gave me courage.)

He fumbled for and lighted a match then, and took a step forward. We had a ghastly glimpse of each other before the match went out, and I saw he was in tweeds and knickers and had one of Daphne's sandwiches in his left hand. He saw the candle then and, stepping forward, he lighted it where it stood on the chair. And when he had lighted it and put it on the table, he actually smiled across it.

"I am not sure yet that I am awake," he said easily. "Please don't disappear. The sandwich seems real enough, but that's the way in dreams. You find something delectable and wake up before you taste it. You see, the sandwich is gone already."

"You dropped it," I said as calmly as I could.

"Oh," he said, lowering the candle and peering under the table. "Ah, here it is. So it isn't a dream! You have no idea how many times I have dreamed I was finding money—sovereigns, you know, and all that—and wakened at the psychological moment." He put his revolver on the table, took a bite of the sandwich, and stared at me, at my gown, *and then at my pearls*. I fancied his eyes gleamed.

I did not speak; I was listening with all my might for the car, but I could hear nothing but the patter of the rain on the flagstones outside.

"I'm afraid I have startled you," he went on, still looking at me with uncomfortable intentness. "The fact is, I was asleep. I got in through a window an hour or so ago, after a day and a night on the moor. I had no idea there was anybody here, until you brushed past me in the dark."

The moor! Then of course I knew. It had been dawning on me slowly. For all I could tell, he might have had the Romney under his coat at that moment. I put my hands to my throat for air because, although he was smiling and pleasant enough, everybody knows that the bigger the game a burglar makes a specialty of, the more likely he is to look and act like a gentleman. So, because he seemed to expect me to do something, I unclasped my collar with shaking fingers and threw it to him across the table.

"Oh, please take it and go away," I implored him. "It—it isn't imitation, anyhow, and Daphne says—the Romney was."

"Oh," he said slowly, staring at the pearls, "so Daphne says the Romney was, eh?"

He ran the collar through his fingers as if his conscience was troubling him a little. Then, "I wouldn't care to pit my judgment against that of a lady," he went on without even a word about the collar, "but—I think your friend Daphne is wrong." His eyes travelled comprehensively to the silver on the floor.

"If you don't mind," he said whimsically—(this seems the only word, although—can a burglar be whimsical?)—"I wish you would tell me how you opened that cupboard door. It was locked an hour ago."

"I dare say it was very unprofessional," I said boldly—for he didn't show any sign of trying to choke me, and my courage was returning, "but—I did it with a hairpin."

"Ah!" He was thoughtful. "And—I suppose that is the way you opened the front entry door, also?"

"No. Violet had a key—" I began. Then I stopped, furious at myself.

He dropped the sandwich again and took a step forward with his eyes narrowed.

"Violet!" he said.

It seems extraordinary, looking back, to think I could have mistaken him for a thief when he was something else altogether. But that wasn't the only mistake I made. I could scream when I remember. He was not at all like his picture, and because I hadn't recognised him as Basil Harcourt, who hated The Cause, I had lost quantities of valuable time.

One thinks quickly in emergencies, and women have one advantage over men. They can think very hard while they are talking about an entirely different subject. His next question gave me a cue. He came forward and leaned on the table, near the candle. I could see he was not very old after all—not nearly so old as I had expected.

"I know it isn't my affair at all," he began, half smiling, "but—I am under the impression that the Hall has been closed for some years. And yet—I find a young woman here alone, surrounded by—er—dust and decay. It's a sort of reversed Sleeping Beauty and the Prince. *You* should have been asleep. As you say, it isn't my affair, but—what in the world brought you here?"

(When I told this afterward, Poppy said: "It sounds exactly like him, of course.")

"I came to steal the silver," I said brazenly.

That was my plan, you see. If he would only take me away and give me in charge, he would be safely out of the way and beyond interfering. And the next morning, when everything was over, I would tell my real name and be released, and everything would be over. Something had to be done at once, for, as Daphne said, "to kidnap the Prime Minister would be a coup d'état, but to try to do it and fail would be low comedy."

When I said I was stealing the silver, which was certainly not worth five guineas, Mr. Harcourt took a step back and caught hold of a chair.

"Really!" he said. And then: "But what in the world did you intend doing with it?—if you don't mind the question."

This was unexpected, but I rose to the occasion.

"Melt it," I declared. I thought this was inspired. Don't they always melt down stolen silver?

"By Jove!" he exclaimed. "You *are* experienced!" Then he sat down suddenly in the chair and coughed very hard into his handkerchief. But he made no move to arrest me.

"Aren't you going to give me in charge?" I asked in alarm, for time was flying. He put away his handkerchief.

"Wouldn't that be a horrible thing for me to do?" he asked gravely. "Perhaps it's your first offence, you know, although I doubt that. You seem so capable. And if I let you go, you may reform. Take my word for it, there's nothing to a life of crime. I suppose you—er—appropriated the string of pearls that are not imitation?"

This was unexpected.

"It is mine, honestly mine, Mr. Harcourt," I began. He glanced at me when I called him by name. Then he took the collar out and looked at it. "I shall advertise it," he said judicially and slid it back into his pocket. "If the owner offers a reward I will see that you get it—minus the newspaper costs, of course."

Then—we both heard it at the same moment— there came the throb of the machine down the drive. He raised his eyebrows and glanced at me. "More people after the silver, probably," he said, and picked up the candle. I slipped after him to the entrance hall.

Just inside the door, with a cordial smile of greeting fading into a blank, stood a middle-aged English gentleman, rather florid, with a drooping, sandy moustache and thinnish hair. When he saw me, the ghost of the smile returned.

"I am sure I beg your pardon. A—a thousand apologies. That cursed—hem—the chauffeur has made a beastly mistake. I was led to believe—I— that is—"

He was staring at me. Then his eye struck the banner across the hall, with "Votes for Women" on it, and from there, it travelled to Mr. Harcourt. He had grown visibly paler. He put a hand to his tweed travelling cap, gave it a jerk, and, turning without warning, he disappeared through the entry into the storm. I caught Mr. Harcourt by the arm as he was about to follow, muttering savagely.

"Oh, he's going to run away," I wailed. "And he will take pneumonia, or something like that, and die! I told Daphne how it would be!" Mr. Harcourt ran down the steps. "Sir George! Sir George!" I called desperately into the darkness from the doorway. There was no answer, but Mr. Harcourt stopped and glanced back from the drive.

"Sir George!" he exclaimed. "What do you mean?"

"It's the Prime Minister," I called desperately, "and if you care anything at all about Violet—but, of course, you don't—oh, do find him and bring him back!"

(Nothing but the excitement of the occasion would have made me mention Violet to him. I was sorry on the instant, for Mother knew a man once who had a fainting spell every time he heard his divorced wife's name, and the only way they could revive him was by sprinkling him with lilac water, which had been her favourite perfume. Very romantic,

I think. But there was nothing but rain to sprinkle on Mr. Harcourt, even if he had taken a fit, which he didn't.)

Instead, he turned on his heel and started down the drive. Sir George had disappeared, and the engine of the motor car had given a final throb and died in the distance. Sounds of feet splashing through mud and water came back to me.

For ten minutes, I cowered on that miserable settee, with "Votes for Women" over my head. And I remembered America, and the way I was always sheltered there, and nobody even thinking of kidnapping the Cabinet. The President being the whole thing anyhow and always guarded by secret service men. And besides, imagine abducting nine men! Or is it seven?

After eternities, I heard voices outside, and Mr. Harcourt appeared, half leading, half coaxing Sir George. He had him by the arm. The Prime Minister was oozing mud and he was very pale.

"Terrible!" he was saying. "Unbelievable! Is there anything they won't do!" Then he caught a glimpse of the seven chairs and the gavel on the drawing room table and tried to bolt again. But the entry door was closed.

"Now, then," Mr. Harcourt said to me disagreeably. "Tell us what you know about this thing. It isn't an accident, I presume?"

I shook my head.

"You see, sir," he said to the P. M., "you are the centre—the storm centre—of a Suffragette plot of some sort. I was a fool not to have guessed it, but I actually thought— Well, no matter what I thought. I presume you were going to Gresham Place?"

Sir George nodded and groaned. A terrible flash of lightning was followed almost instantly by a splintering crash. The very house rocked. Mr. Harcourt closed the door.

"This is Harcourt Hall," he explained. "It's in bad shape, but we have at least a roof. I think you are alone?" to me very curtly.

I nodded mutely.

"I fancy the best thing under the circumstances is to wire to Gresham Place, and have them send a car over—providing the telephone is in order."

"The wire is cut," I broke in. And then, like the poor thing I am, I began to cry. I hate lightning. It always makes me nervous.

Both Sir George and Mr. Harcourt stared at me helplessly. And then, still sniffling, I told them the whole story, and how Daphne and the rest would

soon be there, and that I wasn't really a Suffragette;
that I was an American, and I thought women ought
to vote, but be ladylike and proper about it, and that,
at least, they ought to be school directors, because
they understood little children so well and paid taxes,
anyhow.

When I got through and looked up at them, Sir
George was staring at me in bewilderment, and Mr.
Harcourt was smiling broadly.

"My dear young lady," he said, "of course you
ought to vote. And if voting went by general attrac-
tiveness, you would have to be what Americans call a
repeater—vote twice, you know."

(It was at this point, when I told the story, that
Ernestine Sutcliffe looked contemptuous. "We are
not *all* pretty puppets," she said. And I retorted:
"No, I should say not!")

All this had taken longer than it sounds, for on
the very tail of Mr. Harcourt's speech came a double
honk from the drive. Mr. Harcourt jumped for the
hall lamp and extinguished it in an instant. I hardly
know what happened next. My eyes were still staring
wide into the blackness when he reached over and
clutched me by the shoulder.

"Not a word, please," he ordered. "This way, Sir
George! The door is bolted, and we will have time to

get upstairs and hide. There's a secret room, if I can remember how to get to it. Walk lightly."

I could hear Daphne at the door outside, and I opened my mouth to scream. But Mr. Harcourt divined my intention and clapped a hand over it.

As I was half led, half dragged back through the dark hall I saw Violet enter by one of the windows.

IV

We got upstairs somehow, with Sir George breathing in gasps. I realised then that Mr. Harcourt was still supporting me, and I freed myself with a jerk, on which he coolly took my hand and led the way along the musty hall. Once or twice, boards creaked, and the two men stopped in alarm. But no one heard. From below, came a babel of high, excited voices and the crash of an overturned chair. I backed against the wall and held my hands out defensively in front of me.

"How dare you carry me off like this!" I demanded when I could speak. "I am going back!"

But Mr. Harcourt blocked the passage with his broad shoulders and struck a match cautiously. First he looked at the walls, then he glanced at me.

"My dear young lady," he said curtly, "we should be only too happy to leave you—but you know too much." Then, to Sir George: "I must have taken a wrong turn," he whispered ruefully. "There ought to be a wainscoting here. Good Heavens! I believe they are coming up."

We could hear Daphne calling "Madge!" frantically from the lower stairs. And suddenly, I was ashamed of the whole affair: of myself, for lending myself to it; of Violet, for thrusting the man beside me out of her life and then stooping to borrow his house; of Poppy, for braining a man with a chair and then being afraid of a bat. I turned to Mr. Harcourt as the footsteps ran up the stairs.

"The door at the end of the corridor is partly open," I whispered. "We may be able to lock it behind us."

With that *we*, I shifted my allegiance. From that moment, my sole object was to get the Prime Minister of Great Britain back to his family, his friends, and his Sovereign without injury.

We scurried down the hall and closed the door behind us. It did not lock! But there was no time to go elsewhere. We stood just inside the door, breathing hard, and listened. For a time, the search confined itself to the lower floor. Mr. Harcourt struck another match and looked around him.

We were in a huge, old-fashioned bedroom with mullioned windows and panelled walls. The furniture was carefully covered, and the carpet had been folded and wrapped in the centre of the floor. I sat down on it in a perfectly exhausted condition.

Mr. Harcourt stood with his back against the door, and we all listened. But the search had not penetrated to our wing. Sir George was breathing heavily and mopping his head. The air was stifling.

"I'm awfully sorry," said Mr. Harcourt cautiously; "I could have sworn I had taken the right turn. If I remember rightly there was a passage from the Refuge Chamber down to the garden. How many women are downstairs?"

"Six," I whispered, "and I suppose Poppy Stafford would count as two. She almost killed a man last year." When Sir George heard Poppy's name, he began to fumble with the window lock. "And, of course," I went on, "your—I mean—Violet knows the house perfectly."

"If we could get out of here," Mr. Harcourt reflected, "we could get down to the lodge somehow.

Then, when the motor comes back, we could stop it at the gates—have them closed, you know—and when the chauffeur gets out to open them, steal the car."

Sir George relaxed perceptibly. "A valuable suggestion," he said almost cheerfully. But suddenly, I had turned cold.

"Most valuable," I said from the darkness, "save for one thing: Mr. Harcourt has forgotten, no doubt, but there are no gates at the lodge!"

He gave a quick movement in the darkness. "Then we will have to manage without gates," he said quite calmly. "I had forgotten, for the moment, that they had been taken down. What's the conundrum? When is a gate not a gate?"

But his lightness did not reassure me. Why had he taken the wrong turning in his own house? And what man in his senses would forget whether his own lodge had gates or not! But there was no time to puzzle it out. The search had abandoned the first floor and was coming up the stairs. The Prime Minister threw open the window. From down the hall came a babel of voices and Daphne's soapbox and monument voice. "I think I had better tell you," she was saying "that Violet and I have found traces of two men—muddy footprints that lead up the stairs. Bagsby says he brought Sir George alone. I do not hazard a guess, but—something unforeseen has happened. I only hope—" Here she broke off, and there was a rattle of metallic objects that sounded like brass fire-irons.

The search came our way slowly but certainly. I sat on my carpet and shivered. Mr. Harcourt stood braced against the door, and Sir George had got the window open and was testing the roof of a conservatory with his foot. Footsteps came down the hall, and we sat motionless. I remembered, suddenly, that somebody always sneezed at crises like these, and then I realised, inevitably, that I was going to be the person. Somewhere, I had heard that if you hold your breath and swallow at the psychological moment, you may sneeze silently. So I tried it in desperation and almost strangled, and felt very queer about the ears for an hour after. And at the best, there was some sound, for the footsteps outside turned and ran toward the stairs, where there was a hurried colloquy.

At that, Sir George put the other foot over the windowsill, and in a moment, we were all in headlong flight. Luckily, the very top of the conservatory was boarded on top of the glass, but it began to slope sooner than I had expected, and I lost my hold

on Sir George's hand and slid without warning. I
landed on the ground below, standing up to my waist
in shrubbery and very much jarred. Sir George was
not so lucky. He put a foot through a pane of glass
with a terrible crash, and it took all of Mr. Harcourt's
strength to release him. Standing below, I could see a
flare of light in the room we had just left, and the
silhouettes of the two men struggling on the roof.
Somebody came to the window just as we were
united on the soggy ground. I think it was Violet,
but the crash of the rain on the glass of the conservatory had covered the noise of our escape. Mr.
Harcourt picked me out of my bush, and we darted
into the shrubbery.

V

I have only a sketchy recollection of what followed. The rain beat on my face and my bare
shoulders; the drive was a river. Once, someone
came to the entry door of the Hall behind us and
waved a lamp, which the wind promptly extinguished. And on either side of me, in gloomy
silence, ploughed the Prime Minister and Mr.
Harcourt. Once, Sir George left the drive, seeking
better walking on the turf, and came back after a
moment with a brief statement that he had col-
lided with a tree and had loosened a tooth. And
twice, Mr. Harcourt touched my elbow to guide me
and I shook him off.

He got into the gatekeeper's house through a window and opened the door for us. The interior was desolate enough, but it was at least dry. Mr. Harcourt produced a candle from his pocket, evidently from the room we had left, and it revealed two packing cases, one small keg, and a collection of straw and rubbish in a corner. It also showed that Sir George had struck his nose and that it was bleeding profusely. I got a glimpse, too, of the wreck of my gown, and that and the blood together brought my responsibility for the whole thing home to me. I sat down on the keg and buried my face in my hands.

When I looked up again, a fire was crackling on the hearth, and Sir George's boots were steaming in front of it. Mr. Harcourt had taken off his coat and was drying it. The smell of wet woollen cloth filled the air. He smiled at me over his shoulder.

"This is for you," he said cheerfully. "Go into the back room and strip off that draggled gown and put this on."

"I'm very well as I am," I said, and shivered.

"Nonsense!" He came over to me and held out the coat. "That white satin is saturated. Don't be idiotic. This is certainly no time to stand on propriety."

"I—I can't," I stammered.

"Now, look here," he persisted. "I've got sisters—lots of 'em, and Sir George is a grandfather. Put this on over your petticoat."

Now, of course, anybody who knows anything about clothing today knows that petticoats don't belong with it. And even if they did, there were about eighty-seven hooks on the back of my gown, and only four that I could reach.

"I am very comfortable as I am," I said stubbornly. "Please don't bother about me. I shan't make any change."

He flung the coat angrily on to a box and turned his back squarely on me. It was maddening to have him think me some prudish little schoolgirl who would say limbs for legs, and who, after showing them for years in very short frocks, suddenly puts on her first long gown and is for denying she has any limbs—that is, legs. Sir George sneezed and drew a long, shuddering breath.

"Terrible!" he said. "This is what comes of admitting women to the universities. Would any man in his senses believe that such a situation as this is real?"

Nobody answered. Sir George was inspecting the inner room. I had gone to the window, and after a moment, Mr. Harcourt joined me there. The thunder, which had ceased, was commencing again, and a

blue-white flash threw out the landscape. It showed a
long stretch of country road, running with mad little
streams of yellow water, the drive curving past and
flowing a dignified tributary into the lane, and it revealed something else. *The lodge gates were there, opened
back against the shrubbery!* Under cover of the noise I
turned to my companion.

"Who are you?" I demanded under my breath.
"You are not Basil Harcourt! You had no more right
to be in that house than I had."

"Save the right of sanctuary," he returned, looking at me oddly. "I got in through the chapel. And
what does it matter, anyhow? It is enough for me just
now that you are you and I am I."

"You are flippant," I retorted cautiously. "Why
did you say you had had the gates taken down when
they are still there, opened against the hedge?"

"Jove! That's a piece of luck," he exclaimed,
without troubling to explain. "Why in the world did
you say there were no gates?"

He opened the door and ran out into the storm.
A moment later, I saw him testing the hinges, and I
flung away from the window. Before he came back,
he had closed the outer shutters.

Sir George had taken off his mackintosh and cap
and, with a candle and a deck of cards, was preparing

for solitaire on the top of the keg. The candlelight struck full on his face and showed his sandy moustache hanging limp and dejected, while little beads of moisture showed between the thin hair brushed across the top of his head. He was more nervous than he would have had us know, and the hands—very fine, long-fingered hands they were—that laid out the cards were trembling noticeably. At every sound, he raised his head and stared at the door, and his arched, patrician nose would have been pinched if it had not been so swollen. I shuddered with remorse every time I looked at him. His right trouser was torn to ribbons from the knee down, and soon after our arrival, he had disappeared into the rear room and emerged, bandaged with his spare handkerchiefs, and limping.

We sat there for two hours, Sir George pretending to play, I huddled on a box by the fire, and The Unknown across the hearth from me, stretched on the floor, and leaning on his elbows and whistling softly. Sometimes, he looked at me and sometimes at the fire, and once or twice, I found him watching Sir George with a curiously meditative gaze. I could not help wondering if he was thinking what a chance for ransom there would be if he could hold the two of us prisoner for a time.

(For story purposes, it is a pity he did not. What a novel it would have made! The whole House of Lords out searching for us, and the Premier and myself living in a cave, with our captor sitting at the entrance with a gun across his knees!)

After two hours of cards and steaming before the fire, Sir George became drowsy. He yawned prodigiously, apologised to me thickly, and when the candle finally burned out, he put his head on top of the keg and was asleep immediately. Not a sound had come from the Hall; everything was quiet except for a drip from the leaking roof that splashed in a corner.

Then:

"If you please," I said in a small voice, "may I have my necklace now?"

The Unknown turned quickly and glanced at Sir George, but he was noisily asleep. Then he edged over along the hearth until he was almost at my feet.

"I was going to advertise them," he said in an undertone. "Possibly you recall my fair offer. Some poor woman is probably having a serious illness at this minute because her pearls have been—er—appropriated."

"I don't feel a particle ill," I said stubbornly, "but I want them back. They belong to me. What are you going to do with them?"

"'Melt them down and sell them,'" he quoted easily. "Or dissolve them in vinegar and swallow them. That's historic, anyhow."

"There is a better Biblical precedent," I said and stopped, furious at myself. He was an ordinary highwayman masquerading as a gentleman, and for all I knew, he might at that very minute have had the stolen Romney sewed around him like a cuirass. (He *did* hold himself very erect, now I thought of it.) And I had allowed his debonair manner to carry me away.

But he did not give me a chance to snub him, for the next moment, he was speaking gravely in an undertone and looking directly in my eyes. I will say he had a most misleadingly frank expression.

"I will give them to you when you are safely back at Ivry," he said, "and not one moment before. I am sure Sir George would agree with me that they are too valuable for a young girl to wear under the circumstances. I will give you my word, if it is worth anything to you."

"And if I will not take it?"

"It would make no difference," he replied imperturbably, and leaned over to replenish the fire.

Sir George slept on noisily; the drip in the corner had become a splash; my white satin slippers before the fire were drying into limp shapelessness.

The man in tweeds on the floor raised himself into a sitting position and listened, his hands clasped about his knees.

(Knickers with a man are like décolletage with a woman, only to be worn by the elect. Mother wishes me to cut this out, because she says this story is to be read by young persons. But the modern young person is really awfully sophisticated. Sometimes I feel as though mother is a mere child, compared to me.)

After a time, the man in knickers who was one of the elect dropped on his elbow and began to talk again, looking into the fire.

"Rum affair altogether, isn't it?" he said chattily. "Nature having a spasm outside, half a dozen lady votaries of the vote having spasms up at the house, the—er—Premier of Great Britain, on whose possessions the sun never sets, having apoplexy on a packing case. And out of all this chaos, a moment like this: you and I alone here, where I could reach out my hand and touch you—if I dared—" he supplemented as I straightened. "You see, you have gone to my head. You are the most beautiful person I have ever seen."

One could tell that, however low he had fallen, he had been properly raised—although I think firelight is always becoming, especially with a white gown.

Here, Sir George began to rouse. He coughed huskily, sat up, and looked around him in a daze, and then stretched out his legs and groaned.

"Gad!" he said with a deep breath, "I hoped I had dreamed it." He looked at us both as if to establish our reality, and, reaching over, began to struggle into his shrunken boots.

"If the storm has subsided," he said, stamping his foot in an endeavour to get his heel down where it belonged, "I think I shall be going on. This place is damp."

"Not half so damp as the road," objected the other man. "It's a matter of miles, you know; and besides, I imagine we are going to have another storm. Listen!"

The distant rumble of thunder had been coming closer to us. The rain had almost stopped, but, as Sir George opened the door, over the ominous stillness flashed a terrific fork of lightning, followed instantly by a crash near at hand. A blue-white streak ran down the bole of a tree across the road. The thunder that followed echoed and re-echoed above our heads as we faced each other in the firelight. Sir George had closed the door precipitately, but, as the noise died away, he jammed his cap over his ears and resolutely prepared for flight.

Argument had no effect on him. Whatever had caused his sudden change of mind, he was determined to leave at once. I was panic-stricken. He had been my patent of respectability, so far in what was, to say the least, an unconventional situation. But to have him go like that and leave me there with an ordinary thief, even if he did look like a Greek god except his nose, which was modern—(I do not like those old Greek noses, anyhow; they begin so far up on the forehead)—to have him leave me like that was dreadful.

However, there came an interruption just then, a splashing of horses' feet along the road and the sound of men's voices. They halted just outside the gates, and we caught a word here and there: "Gresham Place," and "Automobile," and one sentence that stuck in my mind and brought me a picture of myself in a hideous prison cap, sewing bags. It was: "Half a dozen are watching Ivry Manor House!"

I think Sir George realised when I did that it was a searching party for him; he had been leaning against the door, listening. Suddenly, he bolted for the keg where he had left his mackintosh, and picked it up. But The Unknown was before him. He quickly locked the outer door and stood with his back against it.

"I cannot allow you to go out, sir," he said very politely. "Whether those men are searching for you or are hunting for—for someone else, you and I have a duty to perform: we must protect this young lady. In fact, and however strongly you may feel against it, I hope, sir, you will see the wisdom of shielding all the women concerned from publicity. And in this case, it is not chivalry; it is self-protection." Sir George wavered. "You can see what the papers will make of it, sir. That the plot has failed would not check the general excitement; the situation is ludicrous instead of serious. That is the difference."

Sir George sat down heavily and groaned. Perhaps I imagined it, but he looked older, leaner, paler than he had done earlier in the evening.

"I have this plan to offer," pursued The Unknown. "We will get the machine from Bagsby in an hour"— he consulted a handsome watch; I wondered whose it had been—"and I will take you wherever you wish; to Gresham Place, or, if you will feel safer back in town, to the express for London. You can get it at East Newbury. If—if the young lady wishes, we will drop her at Ivry on the way."

Sir George considered and decided to go back to town. He would not feel safe, after this, in the country, and he could wire ahead and be met by—I think he said he intended to call out the reserves. I may be wrong about this, but he gave me the impression that he would never walk out again without a detachment of the Royal Guard.

And so we settled down again to wait for Bagsby—that is, we settled down apparently; actually, I was busy devising a method to get rid of our high-wayman and to secure my necklace again. For anyone could tell that he only meant to get Daphne's motor to escape in and that he would probably dump Sir George and me in a ditch, or cut our throats, or sandbag us, and make his escape with everything valuable on us, including my slipper buckles which were platinum and had my monogram on in diamonds.

If I could only have warned Sir George! But there The Unknown sat between us, with his eyes on both of us at once (if this is possible in anything but a fish), asking me how I liked England and what I thought of wealthy American girls marrying impov-erished foreigners; and did I know that in the Canadian Northwest Mounted Police, the word "home" was practically taboo! And I said I abomi-nated England and that I couldn't understand any kind of an American girl marrying any Englishman,

and where was Canada? He gave up at that and, pro-
ducing a gold cigarette case with somebody's initials
on it, smoked moodily for some time.

Then I had my second inspiration of the evening.
I began to get hungry, and, by stages, I grew weak,
dizzy, and, finally, almost fainting. Sir George was
very mildly interested, but The Unknown was flatter-
ingly so. However, when I said faintly that I had had
no dinner, and that I was sure I should swoon if I
did not have the hamper brought from the Hall at
once, he cooled somewhat.

"You would better try to stick it out," he urged.
"You haven't had any dinner: I haven't had food
for—well, for some time. There's a tap in the back
room: let me bring you a drink of water. You have
no idea, until you have to, how long you can go on
water."

"I am not a boat," I said scornfully. And after a
time, when he proved shockingly distrustful of me
and most unchivalrous, he agreed grudgingly to try
to steal the hamper from the house.

"But remember," he said, turning up his coat
collar, "if anything goes wrong, you will have the
whole shooting match down on us here." (Item: was
he American, after all? An Englishman would have
said "the whole bally crowd.")

I think he wanted to say something to me before he left, but having gained my point, I turned my back on him. He went, finally, but he stood for a moment on the lodge porch, looking back at me. I pretended not to know it.

When I heard him splashing up the drive, I turned on Sir George like a hurricane. It took him some time to understand; I had to go over the part about the pearls several times, and when he finally made out that they were very valuable, he still could not understand how I came to throw them at the other man. Then I told him about the theft of the picture, and that we had the thief in our grasp if we could get him. Sir George's face was very queer. When he got it all finally, however, he wakened up at once. He asked me what the collar was worth, and said young English girls did not wear such costly jewels, but that he would see that they were recovered. And the plan was simple enough. The greatest things in life are simple. I said to him that I could easily see how he became Premier.

The shutters of the inner room were bolted on the outside. We would coax our gentleman in there and lock the door. He would be there, as I said with enthusiasm to Sir George, like a ripe apple on a tree, ready for picking at any time.

It worked to a charm, although the result was not what we had expected. Very far from it, indeed. The Unknown, which is shorter than saying "The Man in Tweeds" or "The Sociable Highwayman," came back in about half an hour, with his cap missing and mud up to his knees.

"Jove," he said, shaking himself, "this is Paradise compared to that up there. The lower floor is a wreck: two of them are asleep, three of them are standing on chairs and talking at once, and a tall, fair woman in green satin is having ladylike hysterics by herself in a corner."

"The tall, fair woman in green," I said coldly, "is Mrs. Harcourt-Standish. It is strange you did not know her."

He whistled and then looked at me with one of his slow, boyish smiles.

"Well, as to that," he observed, opening the hamper, "I—you see, I never saw her in hysterics. It's supposed to make a great difference."

"We need a box from the other room," I said, inwardly trembling. "We have used one for firewood." We had, purposely, and it threatened to fire the chimney. I don't mind saying that I had a horrid guilty feeling when I said it, like Delilah cutting Samson's hair, or the place where Blanche Bates took the card out of her stocking in *The Girl of the Golden West*. The Unknown glanced at the box on the hearth, at the Prime Minister, who was getting out the salad, and at me, feeling as I have just said. Then he turned on his heel, whistling softly, and went into the inner room.

Sir George dropped the salad on the instant, with a crash, and had the door slammed and locked immediately. His sandy moustache stood out quite straight, and he looked very military (or is it militant?). There was silence from the inner room, and then my gentleman found the door and rattled the crazy latch.

"The lock has sprung in some way," he said politely from the other side. "I will have to trouble you to open it."

The band around my throat began to loosen, and, anyhow, if he had been little and ugly, I would not have cared. Why should I condone a crime because Nature had given him a handsome body to hold an ignoble spirit? I went over to the door and called through it triumphantly:

"We are not going to unlock the door, and when Bagsby come,s we are going to send for the police."

(That was the Premier's plan. He would waylay Bagsby at the point of his revolver—Sir George's— and make him take him to the nearest constable.

Then Sir George would get a conveyance and make his escape after sending me on to Ivry. I would not stay in the lodge alone with a desperate criminal, and I did not wish to face Daphne and the rest in their present condition.)

I was not hungry, after all. Everything I ate stuck somewhere in my throat and brought tears to my eyes, and Sir George was not hungry, either. He kept walking around the room and eying the door, and once, he got out his revolver and put it on the box. Finally, he went to the doorway.

"If you will pass this young woman's jewelry out under the door," he said, "we will see that you are not molested by the police."

"On our honour!" I called eagerly. For, after all, he had been gentle with me when he thought I was stealing the forks. (Although, after all, why should he not have been? They were not his.)

"I'll see you in perdition first!" came the sulky answer. I hoped it was meant for Sir George. And after that, there was nothing to do but wait for Bagsby.

VI

We did not talk. Sir George watched the door to the inner room and sneezed frequently. Part of the time, he examined his revolver, which he put on the keg in front of him. He was very clumsy with it; I suppose a Prime Minister has an armour-bearer usually, or something of that sort. Once, we heard an automobile far off, and Sir George ran out to the gates and closed them. But the machine went past, and from the voices, it seemed to be filled with men. I saw it again later.

While Sir George was outside in the rain, I emptied his revolver. It is one thing to have a man arrested for stealing one's jewels, and quite a different one to murder him in cold blood. I had the cartridges in my hand when Sir George opened the door, and in my excitement, I threw them into the fire. From that moment until we left, I stood behind one of the packing cases and waited for the hearth to open fire on us. But for some reason, the cartridges did not explode. Perhaps they fell too far back in the chimney.

(x. E. This would make a good plot for a detective story. Sometime I shall try it. Writing is much easier than I had thought it would be, especially conversation. The villain could put a row of shells on a fire log, pointing toward the hero's easy chair. The hero comes home and lights the fire, and then the heroine, whom the villain loves, comes on some agonised errand to the hero's room at night, sits in his chair, and is murdered. Of course, the hero is suspected, or perhaps the villain jumps from behind a curtain to save the lady, kneels on the hearthrug and gets a broadside that finishes him. You can see the possibilities.)

Sir George was growing distinctly less agreeable. He made another appeal to the prisoner to give up the necklace and put it out under the door, but the prisoner did not make any reply.

At three o'clock, Bagsby came. We hurried out to the little porch and watched him stop the car just beside us, with its nose at the gates. As he was getting out, muttering, to open them, Sir George caught him by the shoulder and held the revolver under his nose.

"Get back into the car," he commanded, "and take this young woman and myself to Newbury. And mind you do it. No nonsense. Do you know the road?"

Bagsby muttered sullenly that he did, and then, just when I was safely in the tonneau and had drawn a long breath, Sir George stopped with his foot on the step and—I think he swore. Then he put the revolver in my hand and pointed it at Bagsby's neck.

"Do you know how to shoot?" he demanded.

"Ye—yes."

"I have forgotten my mackintosh," he explained curtly. "Shoot him if he attempts to start the car." He turned in the doorway to say: "Don't take your finger off the trigger." I might just as well have been pointing the automobile wrench, for there was nothing in the revolver.

Then he went into the cottage, and was gone fully a minute. But the strange thing was that as he went into the house, a lightning flash lit up his figure, and he had his mackintosh over his arm! However, he might have meant his galoshes, which is English for overshoes and sounds like mackintosh. (I know at home I always confuse Wabash and Oshkosh.) While he was in the house the second strange thing happened. Bagsby squirmed in his seat in front of me and said in a muffled voice: "Be easy with that trigger, Miss!"

It was not Bagsby at all! *It was the prisoner we had locked in the inner room!*

"Oh!" I said limply, and the revolver slid out of my lap. He turned cautiously and bent over the back of the driver's seat.

"Everything's all right," he said quickly. "You are perfectly safe; I am going to take you home. Unload that revolver, won't you, before he gets back? Or let me do it."

"It is unloaded," I quavered. "I did it myself. But why—?"

"Sh! Hold out your hand."

I did, slowly, and I felt my necklace drop into it. He caught my fingers and held them.

"Now, will you trust me?" he whispered. We could hear Sir George falling over boxes in the house and talking to himself. "I have been fair with *you*, haven't I?"

"I—yes!" I couldn't say less, could I, with the pearls in my hand? "I—I suppose I can trust you. I only want to go home and have a cup of weak tea and go to bed."

"Good girl!" he said. "Of course you can trust me." And leaning over, without any warning, he kissed my palm, while the necklace slid to the floor of the tonneau beside the revolver. It was all most amazing. "Not a word to Sir George, please. He is upset enough as it is. It is my turn to trust you."

"But I don't understand," I was beginning, when Sir George came to the door of the cottage. At that moment one of the cartridges in the fire exploded, and without looking back he leaped off the porch and into the car. I had only time to pick up the revolver and to point its harmless barrel at the chauffeur's back. I have no doubt that to this minute Sir George thinks that a desperate attempt was made that night on his life. For reasons that I am coming to, I never explained. I am very vague about the next thirty minutes. We passed a man, I recall, some distance down the lane, a man who turned and yelled at us through the storm, and I rather thought that it was Bagsby. I couldn't be quite certain. And after we had gone perhaps a mile, we met the automobile we had heard earlier coming back through the mud. We made a detour, which almost ditched us, and passed them without slackening speed.

The pace was terrific. Sir George and I rattled about in the tonneau, now jammed together at one side and now at another. I was much too busy trying to stay in the car to have time to wonder what it all meant. But I found out soon enough.

The other car had turned and was following us! It was coming very fast, too; and they had taken off the muffler, which made it even more alarming. When Sir George saw that we were being pursued, he became frantic. After threatening the supposed Bagsby, he began to offer bribes. For, of course, one could understand that the position was an ignominious one for any Prime Minister, and that his dignity would be sure to suffer if we were overtaken and the story came out. How many times at home I have sat in a theatre and seen cinematograph pictures of people in a motor being followed at top speed, with perhaps an angry father shaking his fist from the pursuing car. But never had I expected to be playing castanets with the Premier of Great Britain in the tonneau of a machine driven by a highwayman, and flying from unknown pursuers who were chasing us for Heaven knows what reason. Even at the time, I remember thinking what a cinematograph picture we would make.

Up to this point, the story has been mild enough. Now it becomes tragic. For at the place where the car should have kept straight on to go to Newbury, it turned suddenly, putting me in Sir George's lap for a moment, and jounced along over mud and ruts, through a narrow lane. Sir George threw me off ungallantly and yelled. Then he leaned over and held the revolver against the driver's neck.

"What do you mean?" he almost shrieked. "Where are you going, sir? This is not the road to Newbury!" But the car kept on. Sir George was frantic. He demanded that the car be stopped, so he could get out and hide in the hedge. He snapped the trigger, regardless of the fact that had it been loaded, we would have gone crashing into eternity and a tree at forty miles an hour.

Then he commanded our chauffeur to turn around and ram the pursuing car to destruction, although he put it differently. And then, finding he made no impression on the hooded and goggled figure in the driver's seat, he stood up frantically and poised the revolver to brain the man at the wheel.

He was quite mad. It was not courage on my part that made me leap and catch his arm. It was sheer self-preservation. The revolver hurtled into the road. (I cannot find the dictionary, but I'm sure "hurtled" is correct, and certainly it is forceful.)

The revolver hurtled into the road, and Sir George collapsed, with me on top of him. Afterwards, of course, I had chills, because, being the Prime Minister, no doubt he could have me put in the Tower or beheaded, or something dreadful. And would it be *lèse-majesté* to knock over the King's representative?

By this time, we were well up the lane, and the other car shot past along the highroad. But our pace did not moderate, and after a little, the other car found its mistake and came back. We could hear it a quarter of a mile or so behind us. And at that precise instant we began to slow up: the engine struggled for a few yards, began to pant, gave two or three exhausted gasps, and then turned over on its side and died. The next moment, we were all three in the road and running like mad up a hill.

If one knows *where* one is going, and whom one is with, and who is behind one shouting "Stop thief!" it is not so bad. But to have a man you don't know take you by the arm and drag you along through briers and mud toward Heaven knows where, with half a dozen other men just below climbing faster than you can run, and it is raining, and you haven't an idea what it is all about—well, it is not pleasant. And I had lost a heel off one slipper and was three inches shorter on one side than on the other.

Sir George was for refusing the hill and for dodging among the trees, but our deliverer (?) held him tight. Once, in a frenzy of alarm, he did break loose, but he was promptly captured and brought back, with apologies, but firmness. It was easy to see why. He would have caught his death of cold if he had wandered over those hills all night in the rain, and what would have become of England? (I am very glad there are no Prime Ministers in America, and most of the Presidents that I recall would be as easy to run away with as a bull hippopotamus.)

And then we found ourselves at a side entry of what seemed to be a colossal house. The door was partly open, and a man in livery was asleep on a bench just inside the door.

The hold on my arm was released. The Prime Minister, assisted by The Unknown, went up the steps and in through the door.

I struggled up alone, with my lungs suddenly collapsed and yells from somewhere behind me in the darkness. I could hardly lift my feet, and yet I knew I must get up the steps and through that open door before somebody reached out from the black behind me and clutched me. It was a nightmare

come to life. And then the footman caught my out-
stretched hand and dragged me in, the door
slammed, and I sat down very quietly on the hall
bench and fainted away.

(One of the people in this story insists that I
was *not* left to drag myself up the steps alone, and
that he took me up and put me on the bench. But he
was excited, and I should know what really happened. He never even glanced at me.)

VII

I am sure, gentle reader—you can see what facility I am gaining; I would not have dared the "gentle reader" in Chapter One—I am sure you will think me stupid not to have understood the situation by that time. But I did not. When I came to myself, the footman was standing by, very stiffly, with a glass of wine on a tray, and it was easy to see that he knew I had lost my heel and that one of my lace sleeves was gone. When I unclenched my hand and found the necklace still there, and then dropped it on the tray while I drank the wine, his jaw fell. But where he had said, "Will you have some wine, Miss?" before, now he said, "Shall I call 'Awkins, my lady?"

"Don't call anyone," I said wearily. "Or—I wish you would find the—the person who just came in with Sir George." And as he turned to go, looking very puzzled, "Where am I?" I asked.

This really should have been said when I first roused.

"At Wimberley Towers, my lady," the man answered, but he looked at me again curiously.

There was loud talking going on down the hall, and, as I sat, I could make out scraps of it. A man's voice, vaguely familiar, in an even monotone, followed by a shrill, excited one, also masculine.

"Berthold said there was a woman in the car, and that was what threw us off, sir. He's always seeing women."

A cold, high English voice came next and then another, but without the incisiveness of the earlier night—Sir George's voice, heavy and lifeless, yet with an undercurrent of scorn.

"Surely you do not think *that* necessary," he said.

The door was closed again, but a word reached me now and then, occasional raisins in the loaf of my darkness. (This is a better metaphor than I expected it to be, because I was loafing, and the hall was dark!) There was talk about Three Mile Lane, and somebody being accosted at a station, and a jingle of something that sounded like money, followed by the heavy tramping of men along a distant corridor and the closing of a door. Then a machine started somewhere outside with half a dozen shot-like reports followed by the soft hum of the engine. I had a queer feeling of being deserted in a strange place, and it came over me suddenly that I had heard there was a Lady Lethbridge at Wimberley, only they mostly called her Snooksie—English people use the queerest diminutives—and what if she came and asked me what I was doing and how I got there? Or perhaps Sir George would wire to town and bring down a lot of people to take me off to the Tower. The more I thought of it, the surer I felt that this was what was coming. I hoped they would let me change my gown, anyhow—white satin and what was left of bits of lace sleeves would look so queer being carried off to prison. And to think how I had dreamed of that gown, and how, because it was my first really dignified evening gown—all the rest being tulle and dancing frocks—how I had thought I would wear it just once and perhaps meet somebody who liked it terribly and me in it. And then I would lay it away, and sometime later—much later—I would bring it out, a little yellow, and say, "Do you remember it?" And he would say, "Remember it? As long as I live." And I would say, "I thought of having baby's christening cloak made of it on account of the sentiment." And then he would hold out his arms and say, "Please don't!"

I had not heard anyone come along the hall, because I was sniffling; so, when something touched me on the shoulder, I looked up, and there *he* was, just as I had been—well, there he was. And he sat down on the bench beside me, in a puddle, and helped me find my handkerchief.

"I didn't mean to leave you," he said gently, "but there was something that had to be attended to and couldn't wait. Can you walk as far as the library? There is a fire there, and I will get you something dry. We can't go upstairs, because I suppose you don't care to let Blanche in on this?"

"Blanche?" I said, trying to balance on my one heel.

"My brother's wife," he explained. "Luckily, she's a little deaf, and Thad has gone up to see she doesn't snoop. What in the world is the matter? Just now you were quite tall and stately, and now you are hardly to my shoulder!"

So I told him about my heel, and he said he liked little women, and that no person who was just five feet two inches and had really curly hair was ever a

Militant at heart, and that he had always thought young American girls were well heeled. It was an astonishing joke for an Englishman, until it developed that he had been living in California for a dozen years and was only home on a visit. And that his name was John, although he was mostly called Jack. When we were nicely settled by the library fire, and the man had brought me a cup of tea that would have floated an egg, I asked him quite casually if there was a Mrs. John. He drew his chair up just opposite me and leaned forward with his chin in his hands.

"Not yet," he said.

Something made me draw my breath in sharply—I think it was his tone—and I quite scalded my throat with the tea. The fire was very hot, and little clouds of steam began to rise from my white satin.

"I have spoiled my gown," I said ruefully, "and I had such plans for it."

"What kind of plans?" he asked, moving his chair forward a little. "Do tell me. I'm always making plans myself. And pretty soon, when you are dry and the motor is ready, I shall have to take you back to Ivry, and when we meet again—if we ever do, for Daphne is going to kill me on sight—you will be very, very formal and have both your heels."

"I hope you will forgive me," I said stiffly, "for calling you a—a thief and locking you up and— everything. I don't understand anything yet; it must be because I am so sleepy."

"Poor little girl!" he said. "What you have gone through! And as for forgiving you, you saved my life tonight. Why, if you thought me a thief, did you unload that revolver? If you tell me that, I will try to clear up the rest of the mysteries."

"I was afraid he might become excited and shoot you," I returned simply. And he bent over and took my hand.

"I hoped that was it," he said, just as simply. He did not relinquish my hand.

(When I told Daphne the story, I merely said of this: "I dried myself by the library fire.")

But suddenly I saw something that fairly made my blood chill in my veins. On the floor, at his very feet, the firelight dancing on their polished metal, lay a pair of handcuffs.

"Oh!" I cried and jumped to my feet, pointing. "You haven't been telling me the truth. They have given you a few minutes, and then they are coming back to take you away. Oh, don't let them to do it. I couldn't stand it!"

Yes, that is what I said. It was utterly shameless, of course, and no properly behaved young woman would ever have said it. But no properly behaved young woman would have kidnapped a Prime Minister, anyhow, and sat in a strange house while her hostess was asleep, drinking tea at four o'clock in the morning.

When I stood up, *he* stood up, too, and looked down at me. "It is worthwhile having been a brute and a villain," he said soberly, "to hear that. I am not under arrest or going to be. The fact is that two entirely different and—if you will forgive me—nefarious schemes have been under way at the same time, and the lines crossed. You and I got tangled in them and nearly submerged. But that was not accident; it was destiny." He took my other hand.

At that absorbing moment, the footman announced cautiously that the motor was at the door. It was horribly disappointing. From destiny to motor wraps is such a descent.

"Do we have to go right away?" I said.

VIII

It was just dawn when we started, one of the grey dawns that have a suggestion of pink, like a smoke-coloured chiffon over a rose foundation. The rain was over, and down in the valley below us, lay shadowy white lakes of mist. I threw back my head and took a great breath.

"How beautiful!" I said. And he repeated, "Beautiful!" But he looked directly at me. I had a queer, thrilly feeling in the back of my neck.

And then we were flying down the hillside we had climbed so painfully the night before, and were dipping into the mist pools. Here and there, grey shadows moved under the trees and resolved themselves, first into rocks and then into sheep. (My descriptions are improving.) And as we went along, he told me the story.

It seems he had come back from America for a visit, and on the second day of his stay, the Wimberley Romney had been stolen by an expert picture thief posing as a tourist. He had caught a glimpse of the visitor, so when the Romney was missed, he started out at once on the search, taking a motorcycle. The whole countryside was roused, and three detectives came down from London. But he had an idea that he would find his man somewhere on the moor, and he had lost himself there. After a night under a rock, he had found a cottage and got his bearings. But the rain kept him there. He had got as far as Harcourt Hall, when another storm came up. To his surprise, he found the place almost in decay, but the house open. He went in, dropped asleep in the morning room on a divan, wakened by hearing me pass within a foot of where he lay, and followed me. When I threw my necklace at him, at first he was puzzled and amused. Later, he kept it deliberately.

The next part of his story he had secured, I think he said, by sitting on Bagsby's chest down the road, after he had escaped by means of a broken shutter from the rear room where we had locked him. Bagsby had had a puncture, and finding he had no time to go back to Ivry for Daphne and the rest, he went directly to the station. A train had just pulled out, and a man in an ulster and travelling cap was standing on the platform. He said, "The car for Gresham Place, sir"—which is what he was to say— and the gentleman climbed in. But about two miles out of town, he (the passenger) had discovered he had made a mistake, and demanded to be set down. But Bagsby had his orders. He carried him to the door of the Hall on the third speed, and the rest we knew.

"Then," I cried breathlessly, "Sir George was *not*—Sir George!"

"Far from it," he said cheerfully. "Poor old chap, what a front he put up! It seems that after he got the picture, the alarm was raised too soon for him. He cut back over the country to make the railroad at Hepburn, and was overtaken by a storm. He found the Hall, crawled in through a rear window, concealed the picture there—it is still rolled in that carpet in the room where we hid, and waited for the storm to cease. But hunger drove him out. The picture off his hands, he made a break for it, got to Newbury just in time to miss the train, saw the constable and a posse approaching in a machine and bristling with guns, and at that minute, Bagsby said: 'Gresham Place, sir.' From that time on, he was virtually our prisoner, poor chap. He fell in with the plot because he didn't know what else to do. But what a shock it must have been when Bagsby dumped him back at the Hall, after he had walked six miles to get away from it."

"But you?" I exclaimed in bewilderment. "If you knew all the time—"

"I didn't. I did not recognise him until he took off his mackintosh at the lodge. After that, I had two problems: to capture him without alarming you, and to prevent the old-woman constable of the country from discovering us and dragging you and Daphne and all the rest into notoriety. Thanks to your co-operation, it will never be known that a Suffragette plot to kidnap the Prime Minister was foiled last night."

"Then—the real Prime Minister"—I could hardly speak. I was horribly disappointed. I had hitched my wagon to a star and it had turned out to be a dirt-grubbing little meteorite.

"His grandchildren at Gresham Place took measles and they telegraphed him not to come."

There was silence for a moment. We were both thinking. Then:

"I am sure you managed it all very nicely," I con-
ceded, "and I am very grateful now that you saved
my necklace and—and all that. But if you think you
captured *him* without alarming me, you are mistaken.
I shall never, never be the same person again. And as
for the reward, I don't want it. I shall give it to
Daphne for The Cause."

He looked around at me quickly. "To take my
place," I amended. "I don't really care anything about
voting, and, anyhow, I should never do it properly.
They will welcome the money in my place, although
doesn't it really belong to you?"

"I have already three rewards," he said, looking
straight ahead. "The revolver which you emptied for
fear our friend might shoot me, the limp little ball
that is your handkerchief in my breast pocket, and
this hour that belongs to me—the dawn, the empty
world, and you sharing it all with me. Do you know,"
he went on, "that Daphne has seventeen pictures of
you, and that I used to say I was going to marry you?
There was one in very short skirts and long, white—"

"Mercy!" I broke in. "What is that over there?"

The mist had parted like a curtain, and on a
lower road, we saw, moving slowly, a strange procession. We stopped the machine and watched. Daphne
was leading. She had the tail of her pink velvet gown

thrown up over her shoulders and *she was in her stocking feet.* She carried her slippers dejectedly in her hand and she was ploughing along without ever troubling to seek a path. Behind her trailed the others. Most of them limped: all were mud-stained and dishevelled. An early sun ray touched Violet and showed her wrapped, toga-fashion, in the hall banner. The red letters of "Votes for Women" ran around her diagonally like the stripes of a barber pole. Poppy was trailing listlessly at the end of the procession, her gown abandoned to its fate and sweeping two yards behind her; a ribbon fillet with a blue satin rose that had nestled above her ear had become dislodged, and the rose now hung dispiritedly at the back of her neck. Her short hair was all out of curl and lay matted in very straight little strands over her head.

And bringing up the tail of the procession— kicking viciously at Poppy's blue satin train in front of him—came Bagsby, a sheepish Bagsby, loaded down with the hamper, a pail, a broom, and a double-burner lamp with green shades. Even as he watched, he took a hasty look ahead at the plodding back of his mistress, raised the lamp aloft, and flung it against a stone. The crash was colossal, but not one head was turned to see the cause. They struggled along, sunk in deep bitterness and gloom.

And so they passed across our perspective, unseeing, unheeding, and the mists of the valley claimed them again.

The man beside me turned to me, his hands on the wheel. "Are you sorry you are not with them?" he asked gently. But I cowered back in my wraps and shook my head. "Take me home," I implored, "and please don't look at me again. If they all look like that I must be unspeakable!"

"We will get there ahead and wait for them together," he said. "And tonight I shall bring Thad and Blanche over to meet you. You—you won't mind seeing me again so soon?"

"Oh, no," I said hastily. "It—it is hours until evening."

"It will seem like eternities," he reflected.

"Yes, it will," I said.

(For it would to me, and if a man likes you and you like him, why not let him know it? And if he liked me the way I looked then, what would he think when he saw me clothed properly and in my right mind?)

He leaned over and kissed my hands as they lay in my lap. "Bless you!" he said. "I suppose you couldn't possibly wear that gown? Will you have to throw it away?"

"No," I announced, "I am going to lay it away.
I—I may use it sometime."

"How?" He was as curious as a child. "Are you
going to make a banner of it, with gold fringe all
round and 'Votes for Women' embroidered on it?"

"*No!*" I said decisively.

About the Author

Dubbed the American Agatha Christie, Mary Roberts Rinehart was born in Pittsburgh in 1876. The author of more than three dozen novels, many of them bestsellers, she was also a prolific writer of plays and short stories, and several of her works were adapted for film and television. She died in New York in 1958.

To see our other great titles,
visit us at:

BLACKBIRD BOOKS
www.bbirdbooks.com

www.ingramcontent.com/pod-product-compliance
Lightning Source LLC
Chambersburg PA
CBHW020633130626
46552CB00003B/1214